minedition

North American edition published 2018 by Michael Neugebauer Publishing Ltd. Hong Kong

Michael Neugebauer Publishing Ltd.,
Unit 28, 5/F, Metro Centre, Phase 2, No.21 Lam Hing Street, Kowloon Bay, Kowloon, Hong Kong.
Phone: +852 2807 1711, e-mail: info@minedition.com
This book was printed in May 2018 at L.Rex Ltd
3/F., Blue Box Factory Building, 25 Hing Wo Street, Tin Wan, Aberdeen, Hong Kong, China
Typesetting in New Veljovic Book
Library of Congress Cataloging-in-Publication Data available upon request.

ISBN 978-988-8341-64-1
10 9 8 7 6 5 4 3 2 1
First impression

For more information please visit our website:
www.minedition.com

Forest Dream

Ayano Imai

minedition

One cool autumn day, as I looked up from my reading, I spied a rabbit zip by, who appeared to be carrying a sack in his mouth–full of what, I could only wonder.

Curious, I began to follow him. Something small and brown spilled from the sack. When I picked it up, I realized it was an acorn. I wondered where he was taking it, and why?

Over the fields and through a town, I followed the speedy rabbit, who scampered toward the mountains. I hurried after, trying to keep up, gathering the acorns he dropped along the path.

We finally reached a bare, forgotten patch of land without any trees—
nothing but dried-up grass and stumps.
It felt so lonely and desolate.

The rabbit stopped in the middle of the field, and I crouched down to hide. As I watched, other rabbits gathered around him. They all had acorns, and they began burying them everywhere. Afterward, they thumped the ground, gave each other a satisfied look, and fled into the bushes.

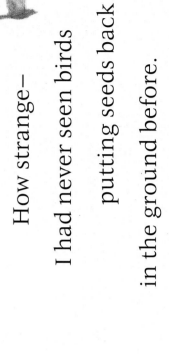

Then from the sky

came the sound of

a thunderous fluttering,

and I was surprised to see

flocks of birds

descending into the field.

There were all kinds of birds,

each carrying a nut

or a seed in its beak.

They buried them in the ground

just as the rabbits had done,

and flew off, calling to each other.

How strange—

I had never seen birds

putting seeds back

in the ground before.

Next a scurry of squirrels arrived.

They seemed to be arguing over who had brought the most acorns.

Then, with a swish of their furry tails, they too dug holes everywhere and buried their acorns.

Once the squirrels left it was very quiet, when a big black bear lumbered out from the distant woods. She placed a bag of nuts down beside herself, and dug a deep hole. Dropping the nuts inside, she took one big paw and covered them with soil before slowly returning to the woods.

Then I noticed a line of insects marching past my foot–a parade of ants, beetles, and flying bugs lugging seeds in their mandibles, heading into the bare field. Some of them even carried seeds larger than themselves!

Watching them made me feel so sleepy, and though I was curious to see what other animals may come along, I couldn't help myself. I just wanted a little rest, and before I knew what had come over me, I was fast asleep on a patch of dry grass.

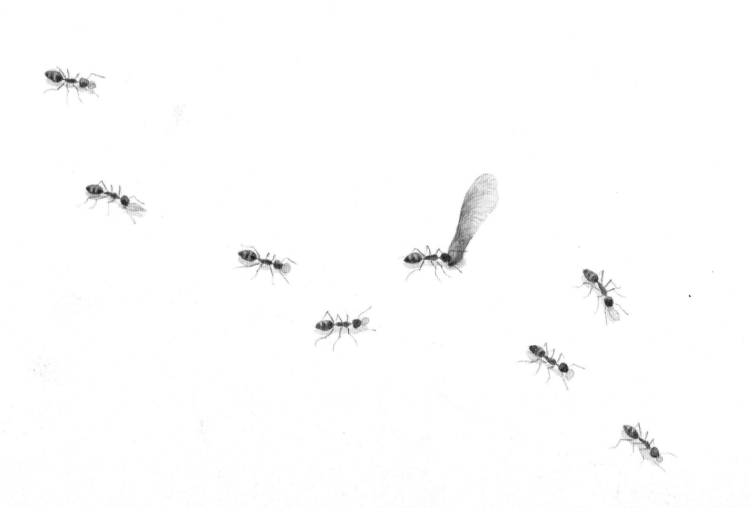

The next thing I heard was the chirping of birds, and when I opened my eyes and stood up, the place had been transformed into a lush forest. What had been an empty field was now filled with trees and glowed green with the multitude of plants and flowers.

Branches and leaves grew before my very eyes. The birds sang songs of springtime, and as the leaves grew even denser, it began to feel like a wonderful summer day.

The seasons seemed to fly by, and as another autumn was about to end, I heard a voice emanate from deep within the forest:

"This is how the forest could be in a hundred years. This is how it was when our grandfathers were young—how it could be when your children's children play here.

"This is where our grandchildren's grandchildren will live—the trees and grass, the birds and insects, the bears and fish, all sharing parts of their lives to make the forest grow.
This is how life continues."

Then suddenly, I woke up from my dream, and the field was bare as it had been before. The forest was gone.

For a minute I couldn't tell whether the forest or the field was the dream world. But in my pocket were the acorns I picked up when following the rabbit. So I buried them in the field, just like the animals had done, hoping they would grow into mighty trees one day...